FREE THROW

BY JAKE MADDOX

illustrated by Sean Tiffany

text by Anastasia Suen

Librarian Reviewer
Chris Kreie
Media Specialist, Eden Prairie Schools, MN
M.S. in Information Media, St. Cloud State University, MN

Reading Consultant
Mary Evenson
Middle School Teacher, Edina Public Schools, MN
M.A. in Education, University of Minnesota

STONE ARCH BOOKS
Minneapolis   San Diego

Impact Books are published by Stone Arch Books
151 Good Counsel Drive, P.O. Box 669
Mankato, Minnesota 56002
www.stonearchbooks.com

Library of Congress Cataloging-in-Publication Data
Maddox, Jake.
    Free Throw / by Jake Maddox; illustrated by Sean Tiffany.
    p. cm. — (Impact Books. A Jake Maddox Sports Story)
    Summary: Since Derek is now the tallest player on his basketball
team, the coach decides to have him play center, but Jason, the former
center, has little confidence in Derek and will not pass him the ball.
    ISBN-13: 978-1-59889-060-0 (library binding)
    ISBN-10: 1-59889-060-3 (library binding)
    ISBN-13: 978-1-59889-238-3 (paperback)
    ISBN-10: 1-59889-238-X (paperback)
    [1. Basketball—Fiction.] I. Tiffany, Sean, ill. II. Title. III. Series:
Maddox, Jake. Impact Books (Stone Arch Books) Jake Maddox
Sports Story.
PZ7.S94343Fr 2007
[Fic]—dc22   2006006076

Art Director: Heather Kindseth
Cover Graphic Designer: Heather Kindseth
Interior Graphic Designer: Kay Fraser

1 2 3 4 5 6 11 10 09 08 07 06

Printed in the United States of America

Table of Contents

Mission BC

Chapter 1

DEREK PHELPS, CENTER

Derek watched as people came into the gym and sat on the bleachers. The fans for his team, the Hornets, sat on one side, and the visiting team's fans from Renner sat on the other. I can't wait for the season to start! he thought. Last year Jason was center, but I'm taller than he is now, so Coach changed the roster.

Coach Taylor called the team over. "Derek, I want you to do the tip-off."

"Okay, Coach," said Derek.

"But, Coach," said Jason. "I always do the tip-off!"

"Derek is taller than you this year," said Coach Taylor. "That's why I made him the center and moved you to forward."

"But he's never done it before," said Jason.

"I'm sure Derek can do it," said Coach. Then he looked at each member of the team. "I'm sure you can all do your job. This is the first game of the season for the Hampton Hornets," he said. "I know you'll make me proud."

Derek, Jason, and the other players put their hands into the circle. Coach Taylor put his hand on top. Everyone shouted, "Go, Hornets!"

Derek walked out to center court and waited for the referee to start the game.

Jason walked up to Derek. "You think you're so great," he said.

"What?" said Derek.

"You think you're better than I am," said Jason, "but you're not."

"I never said that!"

"I'll show you who's great and who's not," said Jason. "Just watch your back." Then he turned and walked away.

Great, thought Derek. I grow a few inches, and our star player hates me.

The ref came over with the ball. He looked at Derek and the center from Renner. "Ready, boys?"

"Ready," said Derek.

"I'm ready," said the other boy.

"Then let's get this game started," said the ref. He threw the ball up into the air.

Derek jumped up. But the Renner center hit the ball before Derek could reach it. Derek watched the ball fly to the other side of the court.

One of the Renner guards caught it and ran toward the basket.

Jason ran past Derek. "I knew you couldn't do it," said Jason.

What a way to start a game, thought Derek. He ran toward the basket.

As Derek reached the key, the free throw lane, the Renner center was already in the air. How did he move so fast? Derek watched as the ball dropped into the basket. Renner scored.

Chapter 2

PASSING GAME

The score was 25 to 14, and Renner was ahead. Coach Taylor had called a time-out, but he didn't seem upset. He was talking to Cody about the next play.

Cody ran back onto the court. The ref handed Cody the ball. Cody took the ball out of bounds behind the basket.

Then he passed the ball to Garrett. Derek ran over to the key and turned around. He raised his hands into the air.

Garrett passed the ball to Ryan. Derek ran up to the low post by the basket.

Ryan passed the ball to Jason. Derek put his hands out, ready to catch the ball. Then a Renner guard stole the ball from Jason. Jason ran after him.

Derek ran to the other side of the court. I can't let them score again! he thought quickly.

As he ran toward the basket, the Renner players passed the ball. It moved closer and closer to the basket.

I have to hurry, thought Derek. Their center is already in the low post, just outside the free throw lane. Derek ran toward the basket.

Just in time! One of the Renner forwards passed the ball to their center.

The center started to jump.

Derek jumped too. He waved his arms to block the shot.

Whap!

The ball flew back toward center court. Cody grabbed the ball and then passed it to Garrett.

I did it! It's ours again, thought Derek happily. He headed back toward the other basket.

It was the Hornets' turn to score. Garrett passed the ball to Ryan. Ryan dribbled toward the basket.

The Renner players surrounded Ryan, so he did a left fake. Then he passed the ball to Cody.

Cody was on the wing, but the Renner players were all over him.

Cody faked right and passed to Ryan on his left.

The Renner team ran toward Ryan.

Ryan pivoted and passed to Jason.

Derek waved his arms at Jason. Jason looked at Derek and shook his head.

I'm open, thought Derek. Jason can see that.

But Jason wouldn't pass. He just jumped and shot.

Chapter 3

CATCHING UP

Derek looked at the scoreboard. Renner was beating Hampton, 37 to 35. They were catching up.

It was Renner's turn to have the ball. One of the Renner guards threw the ball in. Derek turned around so he could see where the ball was going.

A quick pass. Derek ran closer to the basket. Another pass. The ball was at center court.

A third pass, and now the players from both teams were over by the basket. Derek watched as the Renner players passed the ball again.

The Renner player jumped and so did Derek. Derek waved his arms as he defended the basket. Whap! Derek hit the ball away. Garrett ran after the ball.

Derek ran past Garrett to the other basket. Ryan stopped at center court. He turned around to face Garrett. Garrett passed the ball to Ryan.

Derek raised his hands. No one is here but me, he thought. Ryan turned and looked at Derek. Ryan passed the ball to Derek.

Derek caught the ball. Then he turned and jumped.

The ball sailed through the air.

It hit the rim and dropped into the basket. Two points.

Now the score was tied at 37! Derek looked over at Coach Taylor. "Atta boy!" said Coach. Then Derek saw Jason. Jason was frowning. What's the matter with him? Derek thought. Doesn't Jason want us to win?

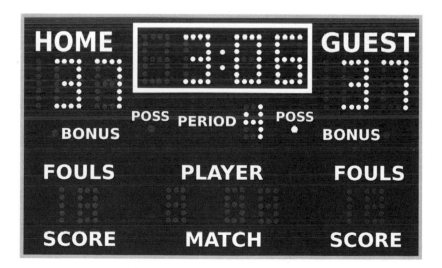

Chapter 4

PERSONAL FOUL

Derek jumped up to block yet another shot, but the Renner center faked his jump. Instead he threw the ball to one of the Renner forwards. Before Derek could reach him, the Renner forward tipped the ball into the basket. Now the score was 39 to 37.

The ref handed the ball to Cody. Cody stepped out of bounds and looked at the court. Then he threw the ball.

Ryan moved in to catch the ball, so Derek ran back across the court. There was only a minute left to play.

Cody dribbled the ball and passed it to Ryan. Ryan did a fake to the right and passed the ball to Garrett on his left.

Derek moved to the low post under the basket. Garret dribbled the ball to the point and looked for an opening. Derek waved his arms. Garrett passed him the ball.

At last, thought Derek as he turned toward the basket. Now we can finally tie the game.

Suddenly Derek was sitting on the floor. All he could see was a forest of legs. The referee blew the whistle. "Personal foul," he called.

The Renner players looked at one another, and then at their coach.

Did they think no one would notice? Derek thought. He picked himself up as Coach Taylor talked to the referee.

Derek walked over to the free throw line. Players from both teams lined up along the lane. The ref handed Derek the ball.

Everyone turned and looked at Derek.

"Don't mess up," said Jason.

Derek looked at Jason. Then he looked at the basket. I hate free throws, he said to himself. Derek lifted the ball into the air and paused. Then he shot it. The ball hit the rim and bounced out.

The ref threw the ball back to Derek.

École Christine
Morrison Elem.
32611 McRae Ave.
Mission, BC V2V 2L8

"Come on, Derek," said Cody. "We need this point."

"He can't make it," said Jason.

Yes, I can, thought Derek, and he lifted the ball up. Derek studied the basket. Then he threw. The ball landed on the top of the rim. For just a second nobody moved. Then the ball rolled slowly off the rim. No basket. Not again!

Derek ran in to catch the rebound, but the Renner guard beat him to it. Before Derek could catch him, the Renner guard made a basket.

Bzzzt! The buzzer sounded. The game was over!

Jason ran up to Derek. "We lost the game because of you! You're making us all look bad!"

Chapter 5

GAME PLAN

For the next week, Derek practiced free throws all the time. He practiced on the weekend and after school. I have to get this right, he told himself.

Derek walked into the gym on game day. I am so ready for this game, he thought. Then he saw Jason.

"Why did you bother coming?" said Jason. "We all know you can't play."

Ryan looked away. He didn't say anything. "Jason, stop the trash talk," said Cody.

"Over here, boys," said Coach. "We have to talk."

Derek waited for the other boys to walk over first. He followed behind them and stood in the back.

"Come on, Derek," said Coach. "I want everyone to hear this." Derek moved into the circle.

"We're playing Curren today," said Coach. "My old friend Coach O'Reilly is their coach. We played together when we were your age, back when the dinosaurs were alive," said Coach Taylor.

"Dinosaurs?" said Ryan.

"Sure," said Coach, "we used dinosaur eggs instead of basketballs."

"What?" said Cody.

"Just pulling your leg," said Coach. "Anyway, I want to win this one." He looked around at all the players.

Jason looked at Derek. Then he looked back at Coach.

"We'll do our best," said Cody.

"That's all I ask," said Coach. He took out his notebook.

"Derek, I want you to do the tip-off again," said Coach.

"What? But he missed the last one," said Jason.

"Give him time," said Coach.

"But I never miss," said Jason.

"Let's go over these plays," said
Coach. "I want to use the two-three zone
defense. Derek, you're the tallest, so stay
right under the basket."

"Sure, Coach," said Derek.

"I play that spot," said Jason.

Coach looked at Jason, "You're the second tallest, Jason," said Coach, "so I want you in the corner on the right."

"The corner?" asked Jason.

"Yes. And you, Ryan," said Coach, "protect the left corner."

"Okay, Coach," said Ryan.

"And you two guards," said Coach, "you'll stay between the point and the wing. Garrett, you play the right side."

"I'll take the left," said Cody.

"Now, let's get out there and show my old buddy who's got the better team!" said Coach with a big smile.

Chapter 6

SHOW TIME!

Coach put his hand into the center of the team huddle.

All the other players put their hands in and shouted, "Go, Hornets!"

Then the ref walked to the center of the court. "It's time," said Coach Taylor. "Let's show them how Hornets sting!"

"Yeah," said Jason, and he punched his fist into the air.

Derek walked out to center court to do the tip-off.

The ref looked at Derek and at the center from Curren.

"Ready to play?" the ref asked.

Derek nodded. "Ready," he said.

"Yeah," said the Curren center.

Here goes nothing, thought Derek. The ref threw the ball up into the air. Derek jumped as high as he could.

But the center from Curren hit the ball away. Not again!

Derek ran to the other side of the court. "I told Coach you couldn't do it," said Jason as he ran by. Derek ignored Jason and kept running. He had to get under the basket!

"Defense!" yelled Coach Taylor. "Defend your zones!"

Derek ran into position under the basket. The Curren players passed the ball left, then right. Derek watched the players weave in and out. Block it, Cody! Block it, Garrett!

But the ball came closer and closer.

Then one of the Curren guards passed the ball to their center.

Here we go, thought Derek. He watched as Jason moved right to try to block the Curren center. The Curren center faked right and then jumped left. He shot the ball toward the net.

Derek reached up and jumped as high as he could. It's up to me now.

The ball sailed over Derek's hands.

Swoosh! The ball landed in the net.

Two points already!

The ref gave Cody the ball. Cody went out of bounds and everyone ran into position.

Cody passed the ball to Garrett. Garrett dribbled the ball to center court.

Derek ran into the key. He was ready.

But the Curren center stood between Derek and Garrett, so Garrett passed the ball to Dylan.

Dylan faked left, and the Curren center moved toward him. Suddenly Derek was open.

Derek reached out, and Dylan passed him the ball.

Chapter 7

DEFENSE

Derek jumped up to shoot the ball. The Curren center turned and hit Derek's arm. The ball fell to the ground.

Tweet! The ref blew his whistle. "Personal foul."

Derek walked to the free throw line. Cody came over to talk.

"You have to make these free throws," said Cody. "We need the points."

"I know, I know," said Derek. "I'll do my best."

The players lined up along the free throw lane. The ref handed Derek the ball. Derek stared at the basket. He tried to ignore Jason. I can't let him make me miss, he thought to himself.

Derek lifted his arms and shot. Blap! The ball hit the rim and dropped out.

"Not again," said Jason.

The ref handed Derek the ball. One more try.

Derek lifted the ball. I have to make this one! He pushed his arms up. But the ball bounced off the backboard.

One of the Curren guards caught it. He passed it to another Curren guard.

The players all turned and started moving toward the other basket.

"I don't know why Coach made you center," said Jason as he passed Derek. "Just because you're tall doesn't mean you're any good!"

"Defense," yelled Coach from the sidelines. Derek turned and ran toward the other basket. I have to defend my zone! he thought.

Before Derek could reach the key, the other side had scored!

Jason ran back to Derek.

"Where were you? You're supposed to be under their basket when they have the ball!" he yelled.

Derek looked at Jason. "Sorry."

"Sorry doesn't cut it," said Jason. "We're here to win, not apologize."

"Look alive," said Coach.

Derek turned and saw that Cody had taken the ball out of bounds. Derek ran back to center court to get ready.

Chapter 8

FAST PACE

The team from Curren loved the fast pace. Derek ran up and down across the court more times than he could count. By the last quarter, the score was 70 to 69, Curren.

Coach Taylor called a time-out. "We have less than a minute left," he said. "We only need one basket to win."

"We won't let you down, Coach," said Cody. He put his hand into the circle.

Coach put his hand in, so Derek did too. Ryan, Garrett, and Jason put in their hands. Jason's hand was on top. "Go, Hornets," they all yelled. And then the Hornets walked out onto the court.

The ref handed Cody the ball. Cody walked out of bounds with it and turned around slowly.

Derek ran to midcourt. We've got to do this right! he told himself.

Cody passed the ball to Ryan. Ryan pivoted and passed the ball to Garrett. Derek ran under the basket.

Cody ran into the key. Garrett passed Cody the ball, but the players from Curren were all over him. Cody did a fake and passed to Dylan. Dylan moved into the wing.

Derek put his hands up to catch the ball, but Jason ran in front of him. Dylan passed the ball to Jason instead. Jason turned around, so Derek put his hands out to catch the ball. Jason shook his head. Then he jumped up to shoot.

The Curren center jumped too, and before the ball reached the basket, the center hit the ball away.

Why didn't Jason pass me the ball? thought Derek angrily. I was right under the basket.

One of the Curren forwards grabbed the ball. Everyone ran to the other end of the court. The clock was ticking down.

Derek ran as fast as he could to the other basket. I have to block this!

He jumped up, and wham! He hit the ball away.

"Attaboy, Derek," yelled Coach from the sidelines.

Cody grabbed the ball, and the race was on. Everyone ran back to the other end of the court. Derek ran back to the basket and waited.

Cody passed to Garrett. Garrett passed to Dylan. Dylan passed to Ryan. Then Ryan pivoted and passed the ball to Derek.

At last, thought Derek, and he jumped with the ball. But an arm came out of nowhere and pushed Derek.

The ref's whistle blew. "Personal foul."

Oh no, thought Derek. I have to make a free throw again!

Chapter 9

FREE THROW

Derek walked to the free throw line. Players from both teams lined up on the free throw lane.

"The game's in your hands, Derek," said Cody. "If you make both of these shots, we win."

The ref handed Derek the ball.

Everyone is watching me, thought Derek. He lifted the ball and carefully studied the basket.

"You're going to miss!" someone yelled from the bleachers.

Derek shot the ball. It sailed through the air and hit the backboard. Then it bounced off the rim and fell to the ground. I hate free throws! he thought.

Derek looked over at Coach. Coach touched his knee.

Knees, thought Derek. I forgot to bend my knees when I threw.

The ref handed Derek the ball. This is my last try, thought Derek. If I make this, we can tie it up. Derek lifted the ball, bent his knees, and shot.

The ball sailed though the air.

It hit the front of the rim and bounced off. A forward from Curren grabbed the ball. The buzzer sounded.

We lost, thought Derek. We lost again because of me! Jason ran up to Derek. "Don't you ever practice?"

"The game's over," said Cody.

"Derek's over too," said Jason. "Coach will have to take him off the team now. He can't keep a player who makes the team lose every week."

"Boys," said Coach, "what's done is done. Coach O'Reilly's team beat us. It happens. But don't worry about it. We'll come back."

"But, Coach," said Jason, "we have a losing record."

"The season's not over yet," said Coach. "We have plenty of time to win."

Coach looked at Derek.

"Son," he said, "I think we need to move you back to forward for a while. Jason can play center for a few weeks while you work on your free throws."

"That's fine with me," said Jason. "We did that last year and we had a winning record."

"Yes, we did," said Coach. "And we will again. It just takes a little practice."

Jason patted Derek on the shoulder. "Just practice those free throws, buddy, and you can be as good as me."

I'm going to practice all right, thought Derek. I'll keep practicing until I'm **better** than you!

Chapter 10

HAMPTON VS. ALLEN

The next week, as he walked into the gym, Derek thought, Here we go. My first game this season as forward, now that Jason got his way.

"Hi, Derek," said Coach Taylor. "Have you been practicing your free throws? Remembering to bend your knees?"

"Yeah," said Derek. "See?" Derek picked up a ball and went over to the free throw line.

He lifted the ball, bent his knees, and shot carefully.

The ball sailed right into the basket.

"That looks great!" said Coach Taylor.

"Thanks," said Derek.

He turned around and saw Jason walk in with Ryan.

"The Hornet's center has arrived," said Jason. He lifted his arms and looked at the bleachers as if he were a rock star.

The Hornet's center was already here, thought Derek. Just you wait, Jason. I'll get my position back.

"Time to warm up, boys," said Coach.

The Hornets did drills as the team from Allen arrived.

"That was a good warm-up, boys," said Coach Taylor. "Now come over here so we can talk about defense."

Derek walked back to the Hornets bench. Jason shot one more basket before he came over.

Show-off, thought Derek.

"I'm glad you could join us," said Coach Taylor as Jason joined the huddle.

"Sure," said Jason.

"Let's get down to business," said Coach Taylor. He showed them his clipboard. "I want to try the one-two-two defense this week. Derek, you defend the point." Derek nodded.

"Guards, you two stay close to the basket."

"Yes, sir," said Cody.

"Sure thing," said Garrett.

"Jason and Ryan, I want you two in the low post. If all the other defenses fail, it's your job to keep the other team from scoring."

"Okay," said Ryan. Jason nodded.

Coach Taylor turned around. "We're ready for the tip-off. Jason, you're playing center, so it's up to you."

"I can handle it," said Jason, "unlike some people we know," he added.

"What was that?" said Coach Taylor.

"I'm ready to start," said Jason.

Great, thought Derek. Go Hornets.

Chapter 11

THE GIANT

The point. I'm defending the point, Derek said to himself as he walked onto the court. I hope I remember to stay there! he thought.

Derek looked at Jason in center court. I should be doing the tip-off, he thought sadly.

Then Derek saw the center from Allen. What a giant! The guy was at least five inches taller than Jason.

The ref threw the ball into the air and the game began. Derek watched as Jason jumped up. But the Giant was too tall for Jason. He slapped the ball away.

Yes, thought Derek. Jason didn't do it.

Derek turned. The ball was coming right at him. He put up his hands and caught the ball.

The Giant ran toward him. Derek passed the ball to Cody, then he ran toward the basket.

"What are you doing here?" said Jason as Derek ran under the basket. "I'm playing center now."

"Uh, sorry," said Derek, and he moved back to the center of the lane.

"Pay attention!" said Jason.

Derek turned and Ryan passed him the ball. Derek jumped and shot the ball toward the basket. It went right in!

Two points, thought Derek. I scored the first two points of the game!

"Why didn't you pass it to me?" said Jason, who was running to the other side of the court.

Why should I? thought Derek. You're not the only player on our team.

Derek ran to the point and guarded his spot. He watched Jason run over to the low post. The Giant jumped up, and bam! Two points! Jason wasn't tall enough to block him.

Cody took the ball out and everyone scrambled. Derek ran back into the key.

Jason ran past him.

"Can't you do anything right?" said Jason. "This is my area now. Go out and get the ball."

You bet I will, thought Derek. As he moved toward center court, Derek saw Ryan catch the ball. Ryan pivoted. He did a fake to the left and then threw the ball right to Derek!

Derek caught the ball. He turned and jumped. Off the ball flew. Bam! Right into the basket.

Yes! I did it again!

"Attaboy!" yelled Coach Taylor.

Jason came over with a scowl on his face. "I'm the center. Pass it to me."

Chapter 12

SURPRISE!

Derek scored.

The Giant scored.

Derek scored.

The Giant scored.

The fourth quarter was almost over and the score was 53 to 51, Allen.

Coach Taylor called a time-out. "Jason, you have to stop their center from scoring."

"I'm trying, Coach," said Jason, "but he's a giant."

"I can see that," said Coach Taylor. "But you still have to guard him." Coach looked at his clipboard. "I think it's time for someone else to play center."

"But, Coach!" said Jason.

"If you can't do the job," said Coach, "then we need to give it to someone else. We're zero and two this season."

"Because of Derek," said Jason.

"Derek has scored most of our points this game," said Coach Taylor.

"He never passes to me," said Jason.

"Their center has you blocked," said Coach. "It's not about you, Jason. It's what's best for the team."

"I know," said Jason, "but—"

"No buts about it," said Coach. He turned to Derek. "I want you to play center for the rest of the game, Derek. Jason, you go back to forward."

"Derek!" said Jason.

"Okay, Coach," said Derek.

"It's the element of surprise," said Coach Taylor. "They won't be expecting us to move our top scorer to a new position so late in the game."

Jason gave Derek a dirty look.

"We're only down by two points," said Coach Taylor. "Let's win this one!"

The Giant had just scored, so the ball went to Hampton.

Cody took the ball out.

Derek ran back toward the basket. I have my job back! Now I have to show Coach I can stay here!

Cody passed the ball to Garrett. Garrett did a fast pass to Jason. Jason passed the ball to Ryan. Ryan turned around and jumped! The ball went in the basket. Two points! The score was tied at 53.

Now the Giant's team had the ball. Derek ran back to the other basket. I have to keep the Giant from scoring.

Just like clockwork, the Allen team passed the ball to the Giant. He came up to the low post, and Derek jumped up to block his shot. Whap! The ball flew back to center court.

"What!" yelled the Giant.

It was a surprise, thought Derek as he ran to the other side of the court. Derek ran to the low post and Garrett passed him the ball. Derek jumped up. Now we can win.

Wham!

Suddenly Derek was flat on his back.

Tweet! The ref blew the whistle. "Personal foul."

Derek picked himself up off the floor. Man, that Giant can hit! Derek's back throbbed as he walked over to the free throw line.

He glanced at the clock. Two seconds left in the game!

"You can do it, Derek" said Cody.

Derek rubbed his aching back.

The ref handed him the ball. "You have two throws," he said.

Derek nodded his head. He lifted the ball and studied the basket. Then he bent his knees and shot the ball.

Clank! The first shot hit the rim and bounced out.

I have to make this second one, thought Derek.

The ref handed Derek the ball again. "Last shot."

Don't I know it, thought Derek. I have to show Coach that I can shoot free throws!

Derek lifted the ball and looked at the basket. Here goes nothing! He bent his knees and shot the ball.

The ball sailed through the air.

Swish! The ball dropped right into the center of the net!

Bzzzt! The buzzer rang.

The game was over.

Game point, thought Derek.

We won! I did it!

About the Author

Anastasia Suen is the author of more than seventy books for young people. She enjoys watching basketball because the game moves so quickly! Anastasia grew up in Florida and now lives with her family in Plano, Texas.

About the Illustrator

When Sean Tiffany was growing up, he lived on a small island off the coast of Maine. Every day, from sixth grade until he graduated from high school, he had to take a boat to get to school. When Sean isn't working on his art, he works on a multimedia project called "OilCan Drive," which combines music and art. He has a pet cactus named Jim.

Glossary

clipboard (KLIP-bord)—a board with a clip at the top for holding papers

clockwork (KLOK-wurk)—smoothly and as planned: "The play went like clockwork."

defense (di-FENSS)—when players on a team try to keep their opponents from scoring

element (EL-uh-muhnt)—the simple or basic part of something

foul (FOWL)—making unfair contact with another player

huddle (HUHD-uhl)—a tight grouping of team members

key (KEE)—the area in front of the basket

offense (aw-FENNS)—when players on a team try to score

pivot (PIV-uht)—to turn suddenly

roster (ROS-tur)—a list of players on a team

Cool Facts . . .

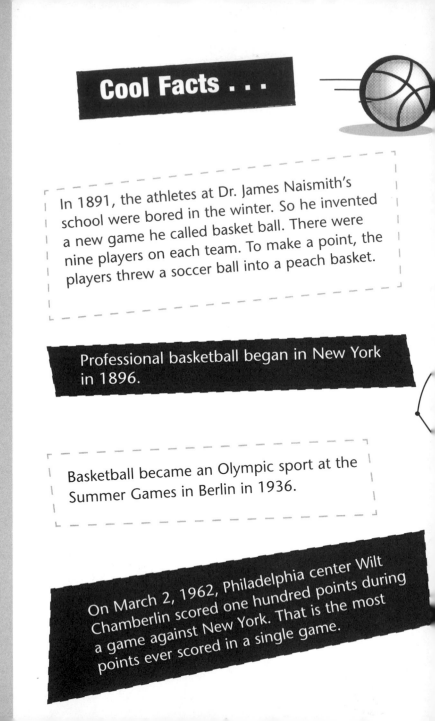

In 1891, the athletes at Dr. James Naismith's school were bored in the winter. So he invented a new game he called basket ball. There were nine players on each team. To make a point, the players threw a soccer ball into a peach basket.

Professional basketball began in New York in 1896.

Basketball became an Olympic sport at the Summer Games in Berlin in 1936.

On March 2, 1962, Philadelphia center Wilt Chamberlin scored one hundred points during a game against New York. That is the most points ever scored in a single game.

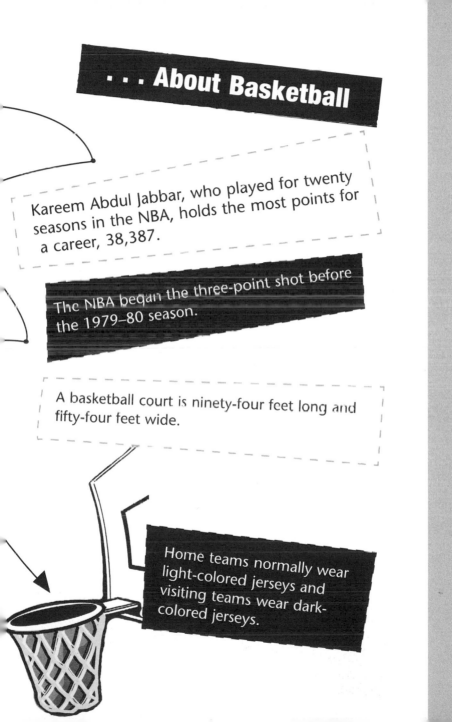

... About Basketball

Kareem Abdul Jabbar, who played for twenty seasons in the NBA, holds the most points for a career, 38,387.

The NBA began the three-point shot before the 1979–80 season.

A basketball court is ninety-four feet long and fifty-four feet wide.

Home teams normally wear light-colored jerseys and visiting teams wear dark-colored jerseys.

Discussion Questions

1. What do you think about "trash talk" in sports? In the book, the character of Jason is mean to Derek. Do you think it's okay to "trash talk" the players on your own team?

2. If you were Derek, what would you have done if the team lost because you missed a free throw?

3. Have you ever played sports with someone like Jason? How would you deal with someone like that?

Writing Prompts

1. The main character, Derek, hates doing free throws. Has there ever been something you've had to practice to become better at? If so, write what it was and how you felt after you succeeded.

2. Throughout the game, Derek never tells the coach about Jason and his bad attitude. Do you think this is a good idea or not? Explain.

3. What are some of the reasons the coach kept Derek at center for so long?

Internet Sites

Do you want to know more about subjects related to this book? Or are you interested in learning about other topics? Then check out FactHound, a fun, easy way to find Internet sites.

Our investigative staff has already sniffed out great sites for you!

Here's how to use FactHound:

1. Visit *www.facthound.com*

2. Select your grade level.

3. To learn more about subjects related to this book, type in the book's ISBN number: **1598890603**.

4. Click the **Fetch It** button.

FactHound will fetch the best Internet sites for you!